TURUM:
The 13 virtues

To: Z. For trust in me.

Title: TURUM: The 13 virtues.
2021. Columba Gelves.
Cover illustration: Columba Gelves.
1st Edition.

PREFACE

Virtue ... What is a virtue? Searching in dictionaries or the internet in and in different disciplines we find a sea of information and different definitions, but we can say that they all have, more words, fewer words, a main idea with which they coincide, and it would be this definition: A virtue is a disposition of the person to act according to certain ideals. It is opposed to bad habits, and has great importance for ethical life.

And how many virtues are there? 10, 20, 30, 40, 100, More? And how are they classified? Intellectual, moral, cardinal, theological virtues? So many things are said and written about the subject. However, in this story we will only talk about a few, and now you will know why.

CHAPTER 1

In the world there are many virtues, you cannot even give an exact number. However, in a faraway land, in a dimension parallel to Earth, 13 virtues reigned. The name of the kingdom was <u>Turum</u>.

The virtues made sure that everything in that kingdom ran as it should, that the nature of the people was not corrupted. Although it was not a place without failures on the part of its people, the percentage was low, maybe 5% at the most, because everyone knew that if they followed the mandates of the 13 virtues everyone would be fine and at peace.

Nobility, Purity, Goodness, Generosity, Bravery, Knowledge, Justice, Volition, Honor, Honesty, Loyalty, Kindness, all of them coexisted peacefully among themselves, contributing the best for the kingdom, in case of any conflict, they all sought the best solution , and thus they had worked for a thousand years already. But since nothing can work forever, this case was no exception. 200 years ago there was a strong discontent between the virtues, and although they were able to resolve their differences, there was one of them that was not very satisfied with the situation. And he could no longer hide his discontent.

-Do they not realize it?! The population is becoming more and more corrupt! A couple of centuries ago the percentage of crime and evil barely exceeded 2% and that caused a great conflict between us, of course, except for the eternally absent number 13, that since Turum was founded has not appeared in the kingdom again. Surely, as she takes care of the kingdom and planet Earth all the time, that is why she's so busy as to come and present herself in front of us- Justice said with a certain disdain.

-That's correct Justice, and you know that each one assumed different obligations when Turum was founded, and we all agreed on what would correspond to each of us, and what would correspond to others, and that includes you and of course to her- Knowledge replied firmly, leaving Justice in silence.
-Besides, it's not like the situation is so bad- Kindness said with a soft tone.
-Please! How is it possible that in 800 years the percentage barely exceeded 2% and a couple of centuries later it rose to 5%? It was too much in a very short time - Justice reproached, getting upset again. Kindness only lowered her face, sad.

-They realize? Is necessary to change some things here, we have to be more firm with the people, otherwise, what would have been the purpose of founding Turum and distancing ourselves from

humanity, if after so much effort we were going to end as corrupt as they?- Justice said more forcefully.
-In that, I agree with you, Justice. Things can't stay the same way- Knowledge spoke again.
-And what do you propose? What can we do to improve things? Guide us, Knowledge - Asked Purity afflicted.

They all focused their view on Knowledge, waiting attentively to hear what solution she would propose. After a moment, the leader stood up and spoke.

-I am right that the situation cannot remain the same, but seeing the increase in recent centuries, seems to me that if we continue as strict as we have been with the people, we run the risk of doubling the number in the next 100 years, and so on more and more. Our good friend who flies around our world and the Earth as it is to take care of us, we cannot ask her to leave her obligations, but it is true that a 13th help is lacking in the kingdom, and even if it is risky, I consider that the best for the kingdom it is to integrate FREE WILL. - Knowledge said with a voice of authority.

A silence that we could call sepulchral invaded the space completely, and after a while, the murmurs began. -Are you serious? Is he/she really a virtue? Isn't it dangerous for the people? - That was the most repeated. But of course, there was one who could not be silent.

-What kind of joke is that?! Free will?! We couldn't even call it a virtue. If we give them free will as such, crime and evil levels will skyrocket in just a few years, or in a few months. THAT WOULD BE THE TOTAL RUIN OF TURUM!!! - Justice shouted desperately.

Everyone was silent and hoped that is what Knowledge would answer him, since although they knew perfectly the impetuous temperament of Justice, this time he had left them thinking, and although they did not externalize it, they supported him inside.

-I understand your worry, Justice. But as I already said, if we continue to want to control them as before, the result will be worse than if we give them the freedom to choose for themselves what they want, they will know the consequences of their actions, and with full conscience, they will be able to decide between a good life, free, in peace and happy, or a life of hardship. Let us trust our People. Purity, you firmly believe in the good and pure nature of people - said the latter, heading to the aforementioned.
-That's true, Knowledge, the human being is pure from birth, is the environment and their decisions that define if they will be corrupted or able to find a balance between the 13 virtues, or will we now be 14? - Said happy Purity, and somewhat confused the question, blushing a little.
-Hahaha, Purity. - Said Knowledge laughing in the style of the famous Santa Claus character. And then she said to all the virtues. -The committee will have 13 figures present, and our friend will continue to be indispensable, only that we will let her do her job quietly, we do not have to worry her about topics that we can solve well. She will continue to be the 13th virtue, but as an honorary member we will have Free Will, who will take her place on the committee and perform new functions according to who she is, that none of us 13 can.-
-As you considered, Knowledge. - They all said in unison.
-Then say no more, in three days we will have free will in Turum. And we will all make her feel like home, since this will be her new home. See you all in three days in the Main Plaza to welcome our new Committee member. See you then. - She finally sentenced, and withdrew from the forum.

CHAPTER 2

And so the days passed, everyone in the kingdom was very busy with the preparations for the arrival of the new virtue. They wanted everything to be perfect, the buildings, water installations, electricity, everything shiny and shiny, even a small show had been prepared in which the meaning of each virtue would be represented. It was undoubtedly the great event of the place; even where Free Will would live was remodeled.

The long-awaited day arrived and everyone in the kingdom was prepared for the event, waiting for the sun to be at its highest point for the arrival of the new virtue. Everything was ready, and finally the time arrived (12hrs) and after of the announcement and introduction by Knowledge, Free Will made her appearance descending from heaven, like she were an angel.

She really looked somewhat young, between 25 to 30 human years at best. Although the virtues existed since ancient times, except for Knowledge (who at most looked like 60 human years), the rest of the virtues were as if they had frozen their appearances between 20 and 40 human years, when they decided to take human appearances to founding Turum, each virtue chose the gender and appearance they wanted to have. Purity was the one who seemed younger, although she said that she was a 20 years body, the rest of them had their doubts since sometimes she gave them the impression, both for her physical appearance and for her behavior, as if it were that of a girl of 15, 18 years maximum and exaggerating.

Free Will wore a dress with a quadrate neckline, long with the part of the skirt loose from below the chest line to almost reaching the floor, with long sleeves as well, in sand color with gold details on the sleeves and in the lower part of the dress, it seemed to be a very fresh fabric, 1.65 m tall and of normal complexion, not fat and less exaggeratedly thin, as was Generosity, who was so generous, that many times she forgot to take care of herself to take care of others.

Finally she appeared in front of the Committee of Turum and of all its inhabitants. After that first moment when everyone saw her, they began to cheer for the new virtue. The rest of the Committee, seeing these reactions, felt very pleased and started the show that they had prepared to receive the new Member.

-Very good Free will, be welcome to this, your new home, Turum. And we hope you enjoy what we have prepared for you- Knowledge said pleased.
-Thank you very much for your warm welcome, especially because you didn't have to, but I'm glad you decided to do it. I am Free Will, but for practical purposes, you can call me F.W. if they so decide- F.W. responded kindly.
-Well, it really shows that she is Free Will- said in low voice Nobility to Bravery, who was by her side.
- It is true, if he is so free, for that he must be brave. I like it. - Bravery answered her, giving his approval to the new virtue.
-You always so enthusiastic and with the boisterous, Bravery. I don't know how we have survived being partners for so long time in our duties- Justice said grumbling.
-Come on! You know that Justice and Bravery go hand in hand, we are like brothers. I know you would miss me if we didn't work together- He said jokingly, to relax the situation.

-Better be quiet now, you stress me out with your chattering. The fact that the majority of the Committee has assumed the identity of a woman… Sometimes they drive me crazy. And you who love to play their game, Bravery- Justice grumbled.
-Good, everyone calm down. We all have a common goal, and we must remain united to achieve it- Loyalty silenced them, one of elders, in human appearance.

Both Loyalty and Honor were the embodied virtues as men who were the elders; they decided to occupy 50-year-old human bodies. And like Justice and Bravery, they were very close and did many jobs together. So in general, when Knowledge was not present in the place or time when the others were, those who instilled the greatest respect among the other virtues undoubtedly were Loyalty and Honor.

-Also, the show is about to begin, and remember that Purity asked so much to be the first to participate. And of course, Kindness gave her place- Loyalty continued.
-If for Purity was so important to open the show, it cost me nothing to give her my place and make her happy- said a little shyly Kindness.
-I understand you Kindness, if it is in one to contribute something to the happiness of others, that's what we are for. It was a great gesture that you had with Purity- Generosity seconded her.
-Oh girls! you are a lost cause. That is why Purity, despite being who she is, takes advantage of you. Even Nobility and Goodness put a stop to it. Well, I don't must to include in this situation to Honesty, she is very firm in her decisions, although Purity makes her face tender to try to persuade her. My respects to you Honesty, you are the only one of the women who calms her down. - Volition expressed.
-Thank you for the compliment Volition, but remember that each virtue has its essence, and that cannot be changed, we are as we are. And this is how we make things work in Turum- answered Honesty.
-We better go and see the Purity show, it is close to ending, and talking is the reason why we have not seen it. When you ask us how we thought, what are we going to say? We can't lie to her. At least let's finish watching his presentation- Honesty continued and turned around to see the final part of Purity's presentation.

She had covered the stage of the Main Plaza with different types of white fabrics (her favorite color, her stamp); she did a kind of dance, which they did not see because they were talking to each other. And they only managed to see when she was on her knees or squatting - that was not distinguished by the white flight skirt she was wearing - hugging her legs with her arms and with her head up, and suddenly she got up quickly and delicately, lifting and spreading your arms. As she did this, a rain of dandelion petals began to cover her and fly from her feet, and invaded the entire Plaza. She lowered her arms, clasping her hands as if to say a prayer, and the moment she put her hands together, she was holding a bouquet of white calla lilies, which she gave to F.W.

F.W. looked very happy with that gesture, although it was definitely noticed that her favorite moment was the rain of dandelion petals. Even Justice liked that.

-Wow, the little girl showed off with that, I accept it. She could even be the one who closed and not the one who opened the show, so the rest of us would not have to battle with all the garbage she left on stage- Externalized Justice to the other virtues.
-Justice, you cannot say a compliment cleanly, without finishing with one of your comments- said Honesty shaking her head from side to side.

As Knowledge was up front in front of the other virtues to accompany F.W., everyone believed that she wasn't listening to anything, but at this point they saw how Knowledge turned her face and looked sideways, throwing them glances that left them in silence.

In this way, they continued attentive to the rest of the show, so as not to cause an upset to Knowledge. Later, she took part in the event Kindness, which sang and danced her own composition that talked about everyone being kind to others, it was quite cheerful and catchy, similar to the so-called K-pop, and that she wasn't oriental in appearance. But well, being a friend of generosity (who was) was up to a point normal, although the fact that she dared to dance with how shy she is, was surprising. Now it was logical why she had been talking so much with Bravery in the previous days, was obvious that she had followed his advice.

Afterwards, Generosity participated and made a representation that showed what it is. About a child who had nothing but wanted to improve himself, Generosity sees this and supports the child and creates a foundation that supports other children like him, and concludes that this child is now in charge of that place, continuing the work of Generosity. And it ended with a blanket that had a phrase: "True generosity, in relation to the future, consists in giving everything to the present" (Albert Camus).

Now was Bravery's turn, everyone was very expectant of his presentation. Well, really, all the men's presentations, since them, contrary the women, did not let people know much about what they would show in their performances. And since Courage was only seen from time to time, speaking to Kindness, no one had the slightest idea what he might have planned for his number.

And they must be said that they were right to be like this and not know anything, since in reality Bravery, because he was supporting Kindness, hadn't prepared anything for himself, but it was fine, to be able to see Kindness so comfortable on stage he was overjoyed, as she and Goodness represented a certain weakness to him, but Goodness seemed to handle the situation very well, so he focused on tender Kindness.

Bravery went to the stage, Goodness asked him: -Can you tell us a little about what you will do? -Something very like me, ¡IMPROVISE! - He replied and continued on his way.

The rest of the virtues just kept their eyes wide, surprised (although being who he was, they would not have to have reacted like that), and they did not say anything, since, as he said, it was very typical of him. So, they were not surprised to be honest, but they had the idea that perhaps being an event of such importance, at least he would have planned something, a little thing. But hey, what can you say, he was Bravery after all (sometimes it might as well have been "Temerity").

He took the fabrics that Purity used in her show and turned them into a solid material and of a dark tone and with them he surrounded the stage, protecting the population. And one of the fabrics dyed it red, it stayed with her, as well as transformed her clothing into a colorful purple bullfighter suit with gold details, and a thunderous noise was heard through the streets of Turum. Yes, there was a herd of 13 wild bulls (torada, correct name) that were specifically heading to the plaza, for the Bravery´s show.

This delighted everyone present, since also in Turum, as in the bullfighting shows of the other dimension of planet Earth, no one in their right mind would face 13 bulls at the same time, and alone. We can safely say that those who did not like seeing this very much were to the other virtues, Knowledge in front tried to be calm, but she was extremely worried about Bravery, and F.W. Well, you couldn't tell if her face was of excitement, amazement, panic, admiration, concern, it was probably all that together what she felt at that moment, she turned to see Knowledge waiting for her to say and / or do something, but at the seeing her so calm he thought that everything would be under control and the expression on her face began to relax, and she also looked as excited as the audience.

And he did not disappoint, although there were a few moments when he almost received a goring, he skillfully dodged them, and on time. After 20 minutes of show and to close it with gold clasp, he dedicated the task to F.W. and gave the final stab. All -including the virtues- were pleased, and finally the bulls woke up as if nothing had happened, and withdrew as they came from the plaza. Because bad habits were not promoted in Turum, these events were only held a maximum of 4 times a year, in the change of each season, and the bulls were never killed, they were only slept with the flags (they only had one thin and resistant needle, with the sedative), and at the end of the show they returned to the bullpen, and then they were left free in their habitat. This is why having a bullfight outside of these occasions was so appreciated.

When Bravery returned with the other virtues, he was equally congratulated and rebuked by fellow Committe members.
-Although you could tell the bulls to stay away if that became necessary, what you did was a risk, 13 bulls! What were you thinking exactly? - Justice asked something annoying, while the girls nodded this time, since for them, this time their curmudgeon partner was right.
-I wasn't thinking about anything specifically, just to give a show worthy of the occasion- he replied so calmly that Justice was more irritated.
-You are completely crazy- he said in a hilarious tone Honor to Bravery.

And Goodness arrived on stage, a woman of about 35 human years, with jet-colored skin and stout appearance, although with tough features, she had a sweet and calm expression in her eyes. After so much euphoria with the number of Bravery, Goodness came to calm the atmosphere a bit. Her number, although brief, was very touching.

She simply stood at the center of the stage and said to those present:
-Well, difficult to show up after Bravery. I have come more than anything, to give a gift to each one of you. Because goodness lives in everyone. But for that I need you to pay attention to what I am going to tell you and do what I ask you to do: close your eyes and think of a moment when someone has shown goodness to you, or you have shown goodness to someone. Ready? Well, now extend your hands in front to receive your gift, open your eyes and take it between your hands-

A series of bright light objects floated in the hands of everyone present: earrings, bags, vases, candies, flowers, fruits, necklaces, dedication cards, etc. All, things that evoked those moments that they had remembered, that the instant they touched them disappeared and enveloped them in light and made them see in their minds how those acts of goodness had changed them, or how these had influenced and helped to other people, as they are now thanks to that act of goodness, and those who thought of those who were no longer alive, for a moment, were able to see them again, as an apparition of just a few seconds. Each vision was only visible to the person receiving the gift. It was very moving for everyone.

When they finished viewing their gift visions, the object materialized again in people's hands. She ended by saying:
-"Because every act of goodness counts, I wanted to show you how important it is to be a person with goodness, and how they are capable of changing lives, I hope you liked it"- She said before leaving.

Everyone was on the edge of tears; it was a great detail of Goodness. Even Justice was making an effort to contain himself with his gift: a shield piece from her first armor. Whatever it was that he saw because of Goodness, it was very meaningful to him too.

-"That cunning woman"- Justice said, and nothing more. He was too shaken to come up with any of his other devious comments from him.

Loyalty's turn came, and he chose a staging in which the life of a couple was represented. From the wedding - which he officiated - until when they reach old age together, emphasizing the marriage alliances, and how despite the stumbling blocks in life, they were loyal to themselves and to their union. He finally marks the death of the couple and showed how the children were also loyal to the wishes of the parents. This number was honestly surprised, since this kind of thing was thought more for the girls to represent, but the ending was more like something they expected, still it was interesting to see that he included a wedding in the show.

This number was followed by Volition, who also did a staging, transforming himself into a child with a dream of becoming someone that no one believed he could become, but with time and dedication, that child grew up and finally achieved it. Then Nobility, Honesty, Honor participated, finally it was Justice's turn, he was the last to pass before Knowledge, who would close the event. But no one imagined what happened next.

CHAPTER 3

Justice entered the center of the Plaza, with a replica of his first armor that he wore centuries ago - the only time since Turum was founded that Bravery, Justice, Volition, Honor and Loyalty Left the city and returned to the other dimension of the Earth, and in their human form, 5 years were absent, although while they "slept" their astral form frequently returned to Turum to fulfill their obligations in this way - and with the piece that he received as a gift in the participation of Goodness, he rebuilt in seconds the remainder of your original first shield.

Being in front of both the Virtues and the population, he took off his helmet and headed towards where Knowledge and Free Will were, but speaking to everyone present.

-A thousand years ago we founded this city, to get away from all the pollution from the rest of the world. We knew it wouldn't be easy, but we managed to make Turum the place we wanted. But in the last few centuries, something has happened, and the contamination of the outer world from the other dimension seems to have reached us, and that is something extremely worrying. And our brilliant Knowledge, the best thing that has occurred to her to correct the situation is to bring... Free Will. Without taking into account that more than helping, it will harm what we have built with so much effort. I am not going to join this circus. Inhabitants of Turum, companions of the Committee, it is time to take real measures and prevent Free Will from ending up sinking our city, the time is now. - Justice concluded.

A silence invaded the Central Plaza, nobody could believe what they saw and heard, one of the Virtues was rebelling, it was something unheard of. Knowledge was stunned, F.W. had an expression of confusion and fear, and turning to Knowledge she asked her: "What is happening here?"

-Don't worry F.W.- said Knowledge, taking her hand. Later she stood up and with a hard expression and a tone as calm as it was firm, said to Justice:

-Justicia, that was a decision that we all agreed in the Committee, including you, you were there, in case you don't remember. This behavior is totally out of place, it is not characteristic of a virtue. Please, leave immediately, tomorrow will be another day, you will be with a clearer mind and then we will talk to the whole Committee about what just happened.

-The decision was made by you, Knowledge. I never agreed that this... virtue, if it can be called that, would come to Turum and join the Committee- Justice replied notably annoyed and dissatisfied.

-Justice! Please leave! - Knowledge rebuked him, something very unusual for her.

He didn't move or flinch, he just stood there in the center of the Plaza. A few minutes later, behind him, Volition, Honor, and Loyalty appeared at his side. The situation was getting dangerous, and just when they thought there could be no more surprises, also appears, and giving support to Justice, nothing more and nothing less than Kindness!

And then several of the attendees joined as well. It was at this time that they realized that everything took on seriousness; Justice was also surprised when she realized the presence of the shy young woman at her side, and exclaimed:

-They realize? Even Kindness realizes the mistake that is the arrival of that Woman (F.W.) to Turum- he shouted.

-Kindness, what does this mean? Why do you do it? - Knowledge asked with deep sadness.

-I, I'm sorry, but Justice is right, Turum has become too contaminated in a very short period of time, and people have stopped being kind to others. And if Justice wants to recover the City and kindness can return to being abundant as before, I'm with him.

"You see Knowledge, Kindness understands it, why can't you understand it too?" He said to Knowledge.

-Justicia, it's your last chance to stop this madness, reconsider! - Wisdom insisted.

-I say the same to you Knowledge, it is your last chance to fix things and make the best decision for everyone, or we will have to make that decision- Justice claimed.

-There is nothing to reconsider, the decision remains the same. - Wisdom replied.

-Then we'll take care of it. So it will be. - Justice finally declared.

And other assistants, who were closer to the Virtues and who supported Justice, proceeded to take them into custody. They tried to let go, but kindness somehow, using her magic, managed to make them not resist and give in to go kindly with people. Justice led them to an uninhabited area of the city and out of nowhere; he built a fortress as a prison for virtues. He did not need to reinforce it as much (or so he thought), since the Virtues that had some warrior or fighting nature supported him, only Bravery posed any danger, but leaving the place devoid of any resources that Bravery or Knowledge could use to free themselves, it was more than enough. And of course, blocking the abilities of materializing things from nothing, telekinesis, teleportation or crossing walls and astral projection of the virtues, he made sure that they remained where he had locked them.

-Well, take care of keeping them well guarded, and well cared for, remember that above all, they are Virtues. In this fortress I have blocked their main abilities that could help them escape, but be very careful, do not talk to them or listen to them too much. Remember that as virtues you can inspire people to do acts of goodness, or generosity, for example. And that cannot be avoided. Stay tuned. - Justice said to the 6 guards that he left in charge of the fortress; they simply nodded, without saying anything.

The Virtues were just there, standing locked up, and watching what was happening outside. All with great disappointment reflected on their faces, less Bravery, he was rather annoyed, since they had been partners in many tasks they had, recapitulating everything, remembering more than anything, those 5 years that male virtues accompanied Justice during the Crusades *, after, everyone returned to Turum and less did Justice want to know about the other dimension on Earth, since he was even more disappointed in humanity. So much wrongful death, he said he did not kill anyone, but that he was tempted too many times to do it.

The current situation made him remember that epoch, the armor with which his, until then "faithful companion" appeared, the fortress where he had been locked up with the women (except Kindness, remember), the guards who guarded them, and that men (except him, of course) joined forces again for a common good, although he did not share the same vision, for Bravery it was a betrayal of him and all of Turum, although definitely, personal betrayal hurt him more.

CHAPTER 4

A year had passed since Justice assumed full control of Turum, and while for the virtues that were immortal, it had hardly been a sigh, for the rest of the mortals it had been a period of time enough to resent the new behavior that had Justice imposed with the help of the rest of the men. And indeed, his measures achieved that in that year that percentage was reduced, that could not be blamed.

However, that percentage went from being simple irregularities and some major crime to being mostly serious crimes. There was only one prison, neither too small nor too big. Now one more level had been added, and even the land where the fortress they had captives to the virtues was located was also used as a prison and Justice had to finish the fortress in such a way that it could be used to isolate the most dangerous criminals from the rest of world. Sure, also keeping them as far away as possible from their star prisoners.

And yes, although the number of crimes had decreased notably, the seriousness of their nature had suffered an inversely proportional escalation. And no wonder, with Nobility, Purity, Goodness, Generosity, Bravery, Knowledge and even Free Will locked away, the balance of the city had been completely destroyed. The lack of inspiration for acts corresponding to these virtues altered the population in different ways. While it is true that Honesty (who decided to be consistent and sincere with her doubts about how beneficial the arrival of F.W. finally, was to also support Justice), Loyalty and Kindness to some extent safeguarded the serenity of the people; Justice, Volition and Honor unleashed the most temperamental thing in them.

Once this happens, is difficult to contain them again, since although virtues inspire certain behaviors in people, they cannot make them appear out of nowhere, they only magnify what is already present in people, if other attitudes are stronger and make them tend to commit such acts, those weaker ones will diminish, making it very difficult or almost impossible for them to reappear.

As time had passed and the fortress added more unwanted tenants to its territory, it was impossible to prevent the Virtues from finally realizing the situation, however isolated they were. They realized that there was more movement in the place and that caught their attention.

-What's all that noise? (Footsteps and noise are heard coming from outside, in the distance) - Asked Nobility to theair, hoping that some of the virtues, or the guards would give him an answer.
-It seems that what Justice wanted to reverse has having other consequences that she did not contemplate at the time. - Knowledge assured.
-We are no longer the only ones in this place. - Free Will said.
-That's good news. Maybe one of them can help us get out of here, right? - Generosity continued.
-If they are here as prisoners, like us, I doubt they are interested in wanting to help us in any way. They won't take that risk, except to free themselves- Bravery snapped.

-That is true, however, as in everything, there is always someone who does not agree with the system, not everyone can be so terrible, if we can reach that person, we can get out of here. And fix whatever Justice has done in Turum. It's time. - Knowledge affirmed.
-But how are we going to do that? Justice disabled our gifts in this prison, and the guards have been very cautious not to get so close to us, and the rest of the noise is heard too far away so that

they can hear us and that someone can help us. Even if we all shout at the same time and with all our might, we will only be like a distant echo, like them to us, if they can hear anything. - F.W. assured them.

-Friends and fellow committee members, you are very intelligent women too; I know you will find a way, and you, Bravery, our guardian, will know how to support them accordingly. - Knowledge told them.

No virtue understood very well what he was referring to at the time, but a few days later, they finally saw a light on the road and came up with a mode.

-Guards! Somebody come! Please, I know that where they are they can hear me. It's an emergency- Yelled Generosity.
-What's going on? - Asked one of the guards from a distance.
-She doesn't feel good; they really have to take care of her- replied Generosity
The guards, warned from the beginning by Justice, acted with caution and rarely interacted with virtues, since even human needs - such as eating, for example - did not represent real needs for them, but that, the guards didn't know it, nor did they had been warned of that.
-this must be for food, what they give us is not exactly the most nutritious. And she, being so young, needs more nutrients - Bravery snapped.

With distrust they approached the place where the virtues were, and through the small window of the door they managed to see Purity unconscious.
-Please, she needs attention. - Goodness pleaded.
Not completely convinced, and not knowing what to do, since that had never happened, and Justice never mentioned anything about what to do in those cases. Finally they opened the door and 2 guards entered to check on to Purity. She only opened her eyes for a moment and fainted again, but that was enough, and before the pleas of Goodness and Generosity they were finally able to communicate with those guards, two others had stayed in the entrance and ended up approaching as well, so they could resorting to their good heart and thus they brought forth acts of kindness and generosity, and finally they came out.

Two other guards had remained outside, who did not enter at any time, but Bravery took care of those and knocked them out when they wanted to prevent Purity from being taken to a doctor and they were going to call and communicate with other people. Leaving, they were transported in an all-terrain truck, and they went on their way to a hospital in the midtown, but since they were on the outskirts, in the limits, it was a long way: almost an hour.

The guards drove as fast as they could, but it seemed that they were not advancing - and they were not mistaken, outside the place where they were locked in the fortress, the Justice blockades no longer worked - and what they did was call the hospital and warn that they were going on the way, as well as asking for indications to bring Purity back to consciousness, or at least verify that her vital signs were okay.

At this time the other virtues took the opportunity to speak with the guards, resorting to their act of nobility, goodness and bravery, to be able to make them see why it was so important that all the virtues work together again, and not just a few - as it was in these moments - to restore balance in Turum and for the well-being of all.

-Their honor and loyalty are remarkable, they are so committed to the cause and that is to be admired. However, if you want the best for Turum, and it seems to me that everyone here wants that, it is best if the Committee and its functions are restored. If we have realized while locked up, much more abroad, you know much better the current situation in the city. Do you sincerely believe that things are fine, as they are being handled? -Said Knowledge with a tone of voice that made it impossible to ignore what he was saying, and left you thinking.

After saying this, Purity slowly regained consciousness. And she said to the guards:
-Please, help us, help Turum, I know that it is their truest and purest desire, ours too, but we can't do it while locked up - she said almost pleadingly, while she's sat, restoring her health in those moments, magically.

CHAPTER 5

Now the Virtues could retunr to form the Committee, but for that, they needed the support of the people in Turum, and as fugitives they could really do little. They were free from the Justice's fortress, but not free to walk quietly through the streets. They had to hide away on the other side of town.

Deep in a jungle, following the path of the river, a canyon could be seen, and there, a series of arches, tunnels, caves and waterfalls could be found. The place was really amazing, and ideal to stay hidden, it was one of the portals of the city, in total there were 5 portals in Turum: north, south, east and west, and the last one remained in the building where the Virtues were, the other 4 were natural, they had arisen with the city when they created it, the last portal were enabled among all the virtues, using a little of the magic of the other portals. They all connected with the other dimension of the Earth.

While everyone knew that the portals were in those directions, they did not know the exact location of the other 4 portals; those locations were only known by Knowledge and the 13th virtue. So they were relatively safe, but they knew it was only a matter of time before Justice found their refuge, so they had to act fast.

-And how long will we be safe here, before Justice finds the exact location? - Nobility asked, concerned.
-Not much, but I hope it's enough. He does not imagine that we are in one of the portals, and by the time he considers it, he will have to find the location of the 4, and that will take time, hopefully where we are will be the last place to come. It's all we have now. - Knowledge answered her.
-By the type of place we are in, will be impossible for him to send many people for us, only Justice can pass, and he will have to come with the other Virtues, if he wants to have a chance, and that will also be an opportunity to U.S.-
-That is excellent, Knowledge- she answered with some euphoria and joy Bravery.
-That's right; we equalize the chances for everyone. - Knowledge said.
-Even so, how long can it take him, days? - Purity asked afflicted.
-That's why we have to act fast; time is even more valuable in these moments. The name they gave to this place on Earth from the other dimension is very appropriate now: The Arc of the time. And it is in that dimension that is our only option. - Knowledge told to the other virtues.
-What do you mean? What are you suggesting, Knowledge? - Asked Generosity intrigued.
-We must bring a human from the other dimension to Turum - she sentenced.

Columba Gelves
January-2021

They all fell silent, and then Goodness spoke:
-But how can a human from the other dimension help us that one from Turum can't help us? -
-We need someone totally foreign to the place, and who possesses exactly the 13 virtues, well, 14 virtues, and thus avoid that Justice ends up blocking us again, or sealing our magic. Remember that now he has in his hands the ballot boxes of all virtues. And only someone outside the city will be able to enter the place and take them, and in case of being necessary, open them. - Knowledge indicated.

-Maybe we can support to Free Will with what little magic we have left, finally, her urn is empty, and would not be necessary to expose the city or the human, or the other dimension- Goodness suggested.
-That could work, it's a good idea, we could try it- F.W. seconded
-With the complete magic of a single virtue and just a little more of us 6, it will be impossible to be victorious, Justice has the total magic, including him, of 6 virtues, and a large part of the magic of us 6, contained in the urns - Knowledge landed them.

After much thought, the other Virtues ended up realizing that there was no other more viable option, and more with time running out. Unanimously made the decision, they opened the portal, but not before discussing how they would choose the human in question.

-In the other dimension, they love doing activities that they call "ecotourism" and they come to this place a lot, so let's not worry about the number of candidates. Now, not just anyone comes to this place. So whoever gets to where we are is a person with that special something, and will be the right person, only the right one will go through the portal, trust - Knowledge indicated.

And they waited, but it was not happens immediate. Despite the fact that the time in the virtues did not mean a problem (they are eternal), in this case, and since Turum is a city inhabited by humans with a very short finite time of life (less than 100 years life expectancy) and Justice getting closer and closer to their hiding place, they became more and more anxious and despair began to dominate them. But on the third day, someone finally broke through the portal.

CHAPTER 6

Carmina was turning 18, and as a gift she gave herself a trip. She had been working for the last 3 years on her summer vacation to be able to make that trip, and although her parents did not like that she went away for a week with a group of strangers on a group tour, Carmi - as they affectionately called her - was very stubborn and if she wanted something, she didn't rest until she got it.

She had talked to her parents since she was 15 about wanting to take a trip for her birthday, but because money was not abundant at home, her parents could not afford it. So she made a request: to take a trip on her account for her 18th birthday. And although they weren't very convinced about it, they told her that if she could afford that trip, they would let her go where she wanted. But they didn't think that she was actually going to work so hard and that she would can pay for the trip, so even though they wanted her not go to the trip, they had no choice that to give her permission. Finally, she was already reaching her legal age; they knew that even if they told her that they would not let her go, she being 18 years old, with or without permission, would end up going.

-Take care of yourself Carmi, and you already know that you can call us at any time. - her mother told her.
-You already know that we are here for what you need, and that we love you." - Her father told her.
-Yes and yes to both, don't worry, I'm not leaving forever or for a year, will only be a week and I'll be back, don't worry so much. Also, I'm going with a group, that's not going completely alone. - Carmi reassured them.
-Yes, but they are not friends of yours that we know. - Her mother replied.
-On the road we could make friends, you don't worry mom - She said very relaxed and confident. - Besides, none of my friends could make the trip with me, and I wasn't going to cancel it just for that. The plans have to continue, and when I can make one with them I will, but this trip I had to do it now. I worked hard for it, and you both know it. - Carmi continued.

-Well then take good care of yourself. And see you in a week; we will be attentive to phones and cell phones. We will miss you.- His father told her affectionately, trying to hide the concern he felt so as not to make his wife, Carmi's mother, more nervous.
And the three of them said goodbye with a strong family hug, before the trip coordinator called them to get on the bus.

Carmi got in and said goodbye through the window and shortly after the bus started off. On the road, she felt someone touch her back and turned around, he was the coordinator.
-You owe me Carmi, now just do not think about getting lost in some remote point and please, when we all meet to return you have here to be to return with us.- he said this latter almost pleadingly.
-Yes friend, I owe you one, you know how my parents are. But I promise you that when you are here to back, I will also be here to take the bus with you. Ok. Relax.- Carmina said trying to reassure him.

Really she was only going to travel with them to the first destination and there she would see them again until for to return home all, but she would do her own tour, as she wanted. She had to lie because she knew that if she said that to her parents, then they would definitely not give her permission, and she didn't want to have to escape away. Mean, she was already 18 years old; it was no longer like to continue with those 15-year-old adolescent customs.

Finally she arrived the first point and from there she took another bus that would take her to where her first place on her list of places to visit began (and she did not know that this was the only place where she would stay all week): The Arc of Time. She even she planned to camp there, was the perfect season. Carmina liked extreme sports, but her parents had never liked that, however, for the same stubbornness, and because she was the only child, they ended up accessing many of her likes.

She had already gone to these types of walks before and her parents accompanied her (just watching, of course) and in a recreational center in the city they taught rappelling classes to children, and since then little Carmi, barely of 8 liked her those sports. She was so good that she ended up becoming friend with and protegee by the instructor, who later introduced her to other extreme sports, and as the instructor, she ended up becoming friends with Carmi's parents, as they agreed to let her train her.

The fact that she was a woman helped a lot, if instead of a woman had been a man, her parents would not have had the same confidence in him, because they were a bit overprotective regarding these issues.

But this time she wanted to celebrate her coming to the legal age in style, and part of that celebration was to take a trip of extreme activities, by herself, without supervision. The instructor did not agree very much, she wanted to go with her, for that reason she said the same thing to her parents. She didn't like to lie to her, she was more than her instructor, she was her friend, and she had kept many secrets from her, but this time she didn't seem willing to give in, so she had no choice.

The afternoon was close to turning into night and that is why she decided to camp in the upper part of the arch, although by the season it was possible to camp in the lower part, having not had enough time to explore the place and with the night so close, He didn't want to try her luck too much. So, that night he would stay in the upper part, the next day he would explore much better the place with the sunlight, and find a place lower down where he could install his things to be able to camp the rest of her stay there.

The day arrived and with it, the beginning of his extreme sports activities, or so she had planned. She first he carried her belongings to the lower part of the arc with the help of her rappel tools, and then she went down, the view was amazing, it was a beautiful place. After a few minutes of contemplating the beauty of the place, she continued to explore the tunnels more in depth and find a good place to camp, and then continue with her other contemplated activities: hiking *, rappelling *, climbing * (or mountaineering), tour of the river by kayak *, and if was possible, even though she hadn't done it before: a quiet horseback ride.

She found the right site, left her things and when she was about to leave to begin his activities, something a little further deep into the tunnel caught her attention, but as there were areas where the sun's rays could filter, Carmina thoughts that was what she was seeing, so she no longer took more importance it over and continued with her owns.

And she enjoyed each activity too much, although as for hiking, after a couple of hours she started to get a little tired, after a few minutes of rest continued on her way and reached the end of the haul, she ate something in a small establishment of food from the community she had come to finally. Everything was clearly homemade and very rudimentary, and Carmi loved that, she thought what that type of food was always the most delicious, that is why on the trips she had had the opportunity to do, she preferred to eat in street stalls than in restaurants, the seasoning has no comparison.

After eating and spending a couple of hours in the place, she made her long-awaited horseback ride. Carmi, aware that she did not know how to ride, did the ride accompanied by one of the guides and instructors of the place. It also lasted a couple of hours and at the end, she continued on her way to where the Kayak tours began, although in this kind of tour (as in all of them) they had assigned professional guide instructors for tourists, Carmina told them that she was professional and that her could go alone. The instructors do not very much agree with this, but if the tourist says that's professional, verifies it and also expresses that they do not want to be accompanied and signs a release of responsibility, they have no choice but to agree to the tourist's request. Not without first leaving the personal information in the place for any unforeseen event.

They are not supposed to take valuables on these tours either, but cell phones (and some others) admit them under the full responsibility of the owner of such objects. Carmi only carried her cell phone, protected in a special bag, hanging around her neck, and she went alone to make the tour of the river. Due to the dates the river was not so high, but it had a good level, and it was fine, otherwise she would not have been able to camp in the lower part of the Arc. The tour passed without major problems, the odd stream of water a little stronger, but nothing to worry about.

It was already very close to dusk when she was arriving in the kayak to the place where she was camping, so before the night caught her halfway, she decided to do a bit of climbing and rappelling, when she was going down again to have dinner something that had brought with her(the blessed instant soups, thanks to whoever invented them) she saw again that iridescent light that had seen in the morning further into the tunnel, but it was no longer daytime, and she had not yet lit the fire as to be that light what that saw what she saw.

She hurried, carefully, to finish the descent. As soon as she touched the ground, she took off the carabiners * and harness *, and went to where she saw that light. As the fire was not yet built, the path was illuminated with the light from her cell phone; luckily she had rechargeable batteries for emergencies. Would have been better for her to carry the flashlight she was carrying, but curiosity she couldn't wait any longer and it was what she had at hand at that moment.

Upon reaching to the place, at the end of where the river water came, in front of her was a kind of large glass or mirror, as if it were a wall, which was what emitted that litmus light. She drew her attention so much that she reached out to touch him, and saw her hand go through him, but did not see to where, because her hand disappeared, as delighted as intrigued by this fact she continued to go through the glass. And when she was finally on the other side of the glass, she found a place that was exactly the same as where she was before, but in reverse, like a mirror effect, and in that place she saw that there were 7 unknown people.

Columba Gelves
January-2021

Carmina was confused, she didn't understand anything. But she realized that they were sitting on the ground and that when they saw her they stood up, and one of those people who seems was the oldest (Knowledge) told her with a smile: -We are glad that you're already here! Welcome to Turum! We were waiting for you. -

CHAPTER 7

The virtues were sitting on the floor of the place, but when they saw that someone had passed through the portal, they all stood up. And they met with a very young girl, hardly a little older in appearance to Purity, but with an athletic physique: she was not very thin, she had a normal complexion, approximately 1.60m tall, she had a shapely figure from exercise, her skin light (but not too light), dark straight hair a little below the shoulders in a ponytail, black eyes, large and slightly slanted, pink lips and dressed in a light colored sleeveless cotton blouse, sports leggings of black lycra and gray tennis shoes.

-We are glad that you're already here! Welcome to Turum! We were waiting for you- Knowledge said to the young woman.
-Ehhh, Thank you… And you are? - The young woman asked quite puzzled.
-Sure, my apologies. We are: Nobility, Purity, Goodness, Generosity, Bravery, Knowledge and Free Will. We are virtues. - She replied to her, introducing each one, the group's spokesperson, Knowledge.
-Okay. Well, nice to meet you, but I have to go now. Goodbye everybody! Good night! -Carmina said saying goodbye to the virtues, shaking off her hand and going through the portal again.
-Wait, don't go! - Purity yelled, running towards her, and taking her arm.
-How did you walk so fast? - She asked him somewhat puzzled, turning around when she felt her hand on her arm.
-You have found the portal and you have crossed it, you have been chosen, and only you can help us save Turum! - Purity said afflicted.
-I think I hit my head without realizing it, or something I ate turned out to be hallucinogenic. I have to go, she said, quite astonished, going back to the portal.
But this time both Purity and Knowledge stopped her. Yet now Knowledge spoke.

-What Purity just told you is true. We are Virtues who govern in a city called Turum established in another dimension superimposed on yours, we have existed here for a thousand years, but now Justice, another of the virtues has taken control of the city and there is a high risk that, eventually, in a not very long period, the city collapses and everything is reduced to nothing. We have opened the portal in the hope that someone would find it and be able to cross it. You have appeared, and believe me when I tell you that you are our last option. I'm sorry if it sounds unpolite and unkind of me, but it's the truth, and at this moment, Kindness is not supporting us, so there is some absence of that virtue. Also to the fact that for reasons of time, we couldn't contemplate any other option, neither was not viable. Please, help us. - Knowledge asked the young woman.

Carmina, although she still did not fully believe that what was happening and what they were saying was true, she felt moved for some reason, thinking that maybe they did need help, psychiatric at least, and decided to stay to listen to what they had to say to her . She released her arm and walked a little further into the tunnel, sat on the floor and prepared to listen.

What's your name, young lady? - Nobility asked.
-My name is Carmina, all call me Carmi- She was not going to tell them her name, at least the real one, but it was too late, I had already told them.
"Well, Carmi, may I call you that?" Knowledge asked.
"Yes, of course," she replied.

-Listen, as I told you before. - Knowledge continued. - You are in another dimension superimposed on yours, this city is called Turum, and we founded it a thousand years ago 13 virtues, one of us performs its functions in both dimensions, so there are 12 in the city: Nobility, Purity, Goodness, Generosity, Bravery, Knowledge, Justice, Volition, Honor, Honesty, Loyalty and Kindness. To take care of the place we all formed a Committee, but we saw that it was necessary for a member number 13 to show the face as well, so we invited Free Will to be part of the Committee ... - You can call me F.W.-She interrupted. - ... I continue, Justice did not like that idea, and rebelled the day Free Will arrived in the city. With the support of 5 other virtues: Will, Honor, Honesty, Loyalty, and to everyone's surprise, also Kindness.

He kept us locked up for a year and we barely managed to get that the guards he put us free, and we have come to take refuge here, one of the places where one of the portals that the city has that connects to your dimension, are located in different parts of the planet. But it's only a matter of time before they find us, and it won't be long, they've been looking for us for three days. Tomorrow at the latest they arrive at this site and when he finds us, he will lock us up again and we can do nothing. That is why we need you, Carmi, in the building where we had our Committee headquarters and where we lived, some urns where much of our magic remains stored are guarded, and with those urns in him possession, even if cannot open and use them, the other virtues they can open their corresponding urns, and with that magic Justice will be invincible, since its influence on the population increases and its magic does the same, and ours, without those urns and locked, has only diminished.

-And you can help us, the portal would not have let you cross if there was no potential in you, so because of that, and especially being a human from the other dimension, there is no way that anyone can detect your presence. The security systems are only activated with the population of Turum, as long as they do not see you, you will be safe, because one of the peculiarities of the place is that, although the technology is the same and in some cases more advanced than in your dimension, as a matter of principle, we do not use security cameras, except in the streets with traffic lights and road signs, to identify infractions, apart from that, in no other place are they installed ... -Unless that Justice has decided to install them.- Interrupted again F.W.

That is a possibility, taking into account how the situation is currently, but the Committee Headquarters will remain free of vigilant systems, it is a sacred place, the Oath was made, and being the virtues that they are, even if they wanted to install cameras, they will respect that oath, that I can assure you. Carmi, you have to take the urns and bring them to us, only then will there be any chance of reestablishing the city, and that everything returns to normal. After that we promise to reward you, before you return home to the other dimension. Please, help us to save Turum. - Knowledge finished.

Everything they had told him seemed to be taken from some fantasy book, science fiction, she didn't understand, kept thinking that maybe it was some kind of dream, or hallucination.

-Listen, I'm sorry about what you say is wrong, but really, I can't help you, so, good luck, and I'm sorry, but I have to go. What.... What is that noise? - She was interrupted by some noises that could be heard in the distance of the tunnel, although little by little they were listening closer and closer.

-It's Justice! He already found us! We have to get out of here fast! Nobility exclaimed.

-For now we have to go now, let's all go through the portal- Knowledge indicated to the other virtues. - Free Will, is there a possibility that you can transport us to another place other than the other point of the portal when crossing it, so that Justice does not find us? -

-I could try, but it's not safe. I can transport us to another of the places on Earth where another of the portals is, but it is not very safe, we can get trapped or halfway. It would be easier to being on the other side of the portal, take us all to another point- F.W. replied to Knowledge.

-It would be safer for us, but at the same time more dangerous for the Earth, we cannot endanger the other dimension and at the same time expose the existence of Turum to the rest of Humanity, we cannot hide in the other dimension, we have to remain in Turum. You can transport us to another place of connection with a portal, and cross that portal back to Turum, which would leave us in another point of the city, and we can find another safe place, that does not have any portal, that the other virtues don't know, and stay us there longer- suggested Knowledge.

-But that would be hiding us again, will we live like this from now on? You can't be serious.- Bravery said, annoyed, for the first time since everything had happened. It was not like him, more than Bravery, he felt like Cowardice.

-I know how you feel, believe me when I tell you that none of the virtues are pleased with that either, but for the moment, it is all we can do. Carmi is not ready yet, we have to prepare her so that she can fulfill the mission that we have entrusted to her, there is only one opportunity, we have to seize it, the future of Turum depends on it, and also so that Carmi can return to her world. It will only be a little longer- She tried to reassure Bravery. Free Will, let's try it - and F.W. nodded.

-Okay, let's all go at once, there is no time. But like I said, we may stay halfway; I'll choose the closest place. Knowledge, you will have to tell me where the closest portal is in terms of location, respect to the other dimension, and from there we will return through that other portal to Turum. Let's go! Let's all hold hands and let's go through together on the count of three! 1,2...

-Wait! - Bravery said, and with impressive speed, he devised a way to cause a collapse in the place, and everything began to shake.

-Now yes, on the count of three: 1, 2... - and they turned to hear other noises that were closer.

CHAPTER 8

Justice was quite upset when he learned that the Virtues had escaped. He was very calm, solving daily affairs of Turum at Committee Headquarters, when he received the urgent call from Turum Central Hospital. He was quite taken aback when he was notified of the call, he answered him politely.

-Yes, tell me, what is so important that you ask to speak to me directly? - Justice asked the person on the other end of the phone.
-W .. Well, it's related to to the virtues that remain... in the fortress- the doctor, director of the hospital, replied somewhat nervously.
-What do they have to do with the hospital? - Justice asked, hardening his tone of voice.
-I ... is that they informed us that one of the virtues had become seriously ill, and that they were going to bring her to the hospital, but they never arrived, it seemed important to me that you know, so that you yourself can verify that she was well, if you considered it. - The doctor answered even more nervously on the other end of the phone.

Justice was silent and his face reflected anger, it turned red. And all he could do is say:
"Thanks for the report, I'll check her health." Holding back him anger so it wouldn't notice on the phone (the doctor), and he hung up.

In a few minutes he collected himself and gave the order to go to the fortress where the Virtues were immediately. He did not say anything more, and remained unchanged during the way, as things were, was not convenient for others to see him altered, maybe it was nothing and people would inform to the other virtues and they would worry for nothing, so until not checking, did not want to raise suspicions. But of course something did not fit at all, the virtues do not get sick, of course something had happened, something the virtues were up to, and he needed to know what it was.

As soon as he arrived, he went directly to where he had to the Virtues imprisoned, the guards, seeing Justice, stood up and greeted him.
-Justice, It's an honor, how can we help you? -
-Permission - and he passed the guards. He leaned out of the small window in the prison door and saw no one.
-Open the door - he ordered the guards.

The guards were stunned, and did not react.
"I told you, open this door!" Justice ordered once more, with a rather altered tone of voice. They obeyed the order and when opened the door he verified what he feared so much: the Virtues were no longer there, they escaped.

As fast as he came, in the same way he left the fortress without saying a single word. He also did not notice the nervous guards who expected the worst of Justice as soon as he realized the situation, but he did not even look at them, although of course, getting into his transport he told the manager of the place, using a tone of voice that could well seem that he did not mind that they let the Virtues go free: "Lock up the guards who were in charge of my guests, in the same place where they were, until I say otherwise." And he left.

Columba Gelves
January-2021

As soon as he was back at the Headquarters, he ordered the virtues that supported him to gather and a troop to accompany him to go in search of the fugitive Virtues. The first option that came to his mind was to look for them in the most important places in the city, those where the portals to the other dimension were, they were isolated, safe places that only knew of their existence the virtues. For his bad luck, the exact location of the places was only known to Knowledge, but he had an approximate direction, and on the way, with or without a compass, he would find the magical places.

In the next three days he was looking for the magical places, but in none of the three did he find to the Virtues, but he still had one last place to go, they must be there, surely. He did not want to wait any longer and hurried the platoon that accompanied him to arrive before he finished that day to the place that he suspected was where The Virtues were refugeed.

Almost with night falling on everyone, they were finally about to reach the last portal, he recognized it immediately, since the portal was open, that iridescent light gave away the exact location, although the place was not very exposed, the light was saw enough.

Justice realized how small the place was, and did not want to wait for everyone to arrive at the site, when most likely they could not all enter, and did not want to wait more, he did not see a reason, and told the other virtues and the platoon that he would go ahead.

-Wait a little more, it is the last portal, surely they are hiding there, we already found them, and what is the rush to arrive, now? - Asked Kindness.
"Do you see that light, my dear Kindness?" The portal is open; they may want to hide in the other dimension. Do you really want to involve the rest of humanity in this? It's not safe for Turum, we expose ourselves too much. - Justice answered her.
-You can accompany me, you would be a great support, I need you by my side- he told to the virtues that accompanied him. -The space is very limited, the others will not be able to pass completely anyway, it's better than us that we can, let's get ahead of them- he advised them and he assured them.

-Agree. I will speak with them. - And addressing the rest of the companions, he said the following: - Faithful and loyal soldiers and warriors, guardians of Turum. It's imperative that we get ahead to the place, but do not delay, the city needs you, do not abandon now. - He told the platoon Loyalty.

That being said, the virtues went forward in search of their former companions of the Committee. In less than a minute they moved and reached the exact place and entered the tunnels, they only followed the light and in a few minutes (due to the conditions of the ground and the darkness of the place that was only interrupted by the litmus light of the portal, no they could move as fast as before), as they advanced they heard a louder murmur, until the voices were clearly understandable, there were the virtues.

But not only they had heard them, inside the other Virtues had also heard them, they could not be so silent. Suddenly everything in the tunnel began to collapse: Justice, Volition, Honor, Honesty, Loyalty and Kindness rushed to the end of the tunnel, until they saw the other Virtues.

However, they could do nothing anymore.

Columba Gelves
January-2021

CHAPTER 9

-Now yes, on the count of three: 1, 2... - And something interrupted Bravery, they turned when to hear other noises closer. There were Justice and the other virtues, it was time to go. - THREE! - And Nobility, Purity, Goodness, Generosity, Bravery, Knowledge, Free Will and Carmi crossed the portal, leaving stunned to Justice and the other virtues that accompanied.

Justice and him companions rushed through the portal too, but when that happened, they noticed that the virtues were not on the other side when they arrived. Upon realizing this, Justice went mad and gave a furious scream. The other virtues tried to find the virtues in the vicinity of the place, but there were no marks or any trace of them, only a small camp of some explorer from that area in that other dimension, but nothing of the Virtues.

So after checking the place and taking a luggage they found in the camp, they returned through the portal to Turum. They had to move all the rock that collapsed from the place, but with their gifts that did not take them more than a few seconds (Justice and Honor, in addition to the super strength that all the Virtues had- being even greater in males-, they had the ability creating force fields).

On the other side, Free Will had used part of the magic that she had left and connected the portal to the exit of another portal, so while the other virtues were in The Arc of Time, Free Will, Carmi, and the other Virtues were of the other side of the portal that connected with The Lighthouse at the End of the World.

-Now where are we? This is not The Arc of Time. Where are we? Where did they bring me? - Asked Carmi quite confused.
-We arrived at the exit of another portal, I gave the location to Free Will to transport us, it is one of her gifts. In your dimension this place is known as "The lighthouse at the end of the world." It was an excellent construction so that the portal was better protected. I understand that even a writer of your dimension was inspired by this lighthouse. - Knowledge reported.

Carmi came out of the lighthouse, which was more a wooden house than a lighthouse, octagonal in shape, and there was nothing else, they were on an island. It didn't even look like an inhabited island.
-It's a beautiful place, but doesn't anyone live on this island? HELLO! - Carmi yelled.
"I understand that only a few people come from time to time for maintenance work, for the rest of the time it remains uninhabited." Knowledge told her.

The other virtues also came out of the lighthouse to admire the place where they were, they looked so peaceful and thoughtful at the same time, even Bravery that wasn't to remain still for long. Knowledge would have wanted to be able to stay a little longer in the place, next to the other virtues, but they had to return to Turum, it was not safe to spend a lot of time there, both because they could discover them if someone came by, and because the longer time they stayed, it was time that they lost, to find a new refuge that was well hidden from Justice.

-Very good, Virtues, Carmi, we have to go back. Remember that Turum needs us. - Knowledge told them.

Columba Gelves

January-2021

And they headed back to the lighthouse house, ready to cross the portal again and return to Turum. Although, the one who stopped before entering was Carmi, who was not very convinced. However, after Knowledge's request, although everything still sounded like fantasy and she did not really know what she was getting into, she decided to follow the virtues, and that things were as what had to be, even if she was going crazy. The curiosity was stronger than her fear.

As for Justice, there was no time to lose, he had to find the virtues, and prevent them from taking their urns, since he knew like them, that by having those urns, the previous order of Turum could be restored, the Committee included, of course. And to be honest, he was concerned about what role he might have now, once the Committee was reinstated.

Would he be degraded, being locked up too? Or would they forgive him and have only a symbolic place at the committee headquarters, but his participation would be reduced to as little as possible? Would Free Will or would any of the other virtues have more magic and gifts? Would some other new virtue come to Turum? Who was the young woman who was with them? He until that moment had not noticed that presence, until now that he was seeing and thinking about things calmer.
-Maybe she is the owner of the luggage we found, or not? -She thought to himself.

He arrived back at headquarters, thinking about the best option to guard the urns. However, nothing that was in the Headquarters could be altered, besides that it was a Holy place and the best protected of the city, so subtracting the urns from the Headquarters was completely out of the question, but they would have to be even more protected, and the most guarded place, in case they really decided to go for them.

He did not know how much support Knowledge and company would receive now, and how much of their magic they still retained. He commissioned his fellow virtues to go back to the portals and find out which way they entered the city, if they had returned. Or that they could find their hiding place in the other dimension if they had stayed on the other side. Although he was sure they would return to Turum. And whatever the case, that they would find them.

Justice reinforced the surveillance of the Headquarters and the urns, instead of being in the special vault in which they were always protected; he changed them to a safe that was located inside the main forum, where the virtues making decisions were almost always gathered and where now Justice was almost all the time. Unable to get them out of the building, the safest place for the urns was as close to him as possible.

The other virtues set out in search of the new hiding place for the fugitive virtues, and found the portal where they had been. However, the footprints leaving the small island were lost in the sea, and from there they could not find anything else (remember that the sites of the portals look the same in both dimensions, that is why it was also located on a small island that only had the lighthouse). Seeing this, the commissioned virtues decided to open the portals and search for traces in the other dimension, but they only found footprints on the other side of the lighthouse portal barely in the outside the lighthouse, beyond the flat area of the promontory * where the lighthouse was located there was nothing, but if they could make out tracks that were going back, so yes, they had returned to Turum, there was no doubt about that.

CHAPTER 10

Seeing this, they immediately called Justice, who told them that then they had to find the new hiding place in Turum. It would be a little more complicated, because with no tracks to follow, they were again without progress, they only knew they were back, but where?

And the thought that the gifts of Free Will could give them another advantage had him nervous, although if they had found any footprints on the island, it meant that they were already too weak to take another shortcut without leaving a trace. Certainly the thought of him was not so wrong.

It was true that Free Will had many highly valued abilities, that was also why Knowledge chose her, but she was also much weakened, and knew that they could not stay much longer in the same place now that the virtues who sought them knew the location of the portals and where they were led. But she was the only one who could help them take cover, again.

Knowledge appealed to her again, but she was very weak right now, she had used a lot of her magic to transport them between portals.

-They know that I came to Turum to help them, but right now I don't think I can, I lose magic every time I use it, and without a way to renew it I lose power. A moment ago I used too much, I have almost nothing. - said sadly Free Will.

-There has to be something you can do, or we can do, maybe you can't do it alone, but we can support you in something- Bravery assured her.

-Mmm… there is an option, but I will need Purity and Knowledge. Purity will help me connect with them, but, Knowledge, you have to tell me the exact location of … Atlantis *.- Free Will replied.

- Wait a moment; are they talking about Atlantis, the city that sank into the sea? IS IT REAL?! - Asked Carmi, with wide eyes.

-It exists on a different plane than of your dimension, it is still under the sea, but Turum decided to protect it in its waters, so that no one would disturb them. They sealed that deal with magic, magic that only all virtues united would break, so Justice, even if he wants, will not be able to enter there, if he finds out that we are in Atlantis * .- Knowledge informed her.

-Only is possible enter with authorization, we will have to risk being rejected, but fortunately, for this work of conviction we have the best virtues: Nobility, Purity, Goodness and Generosity. In addition, of course, the excellent argument of Knowledge, which for something is the only virtue that knows, among many things, the exact locations of all the sites that exist. - Free Will reported.

So they went to Atlantis. Knowledge directed her to the exact location, the point of contact was established thanks to Purity, that only she, by her nature, could reach the deep, the exact place, and with the help of Nobility, Goodness and Generosity, open way into the waters so that they would arrive freely to Atlantis. The rulers of that submerged island felt the approach of Purity, which was accompanied, and they communicated mentally with her and company.

-What are you looking for here? What can we do for you? - They listened in their heads.

-We are the virtues: Nobility, Purity, Goodness, Generosity, Bravery, Free Will and Knowledge. It is a very delicate situation, and we need you to give us shelter, please. - Nobility answered them.

-Does it have something to do with the other virtues not coming with you? - Asked the Chief.

-It's very intuitive, master. You don't have to worry, know that there is an unbreakable Deal of ALL virtues with Atlantis, and that will not change. That is why we request your authorization to enter. It would be an honor to receive us in your city. - Knowledge answered.

And finally, they opened the island barrier so they could enter the city. As soon as they arrived, Free Will fainted at the stunned sight of everyone. Some of those present took her to the doctors, when she took them to Atlantis, although with the help of the other virtues, she consumed what was left of her vital energy.

While assisting to Free Will, the other virtues saluted and paid their respects to the Atlanteans* and at that moment the rulers of Atlantis noted the presence of a non-virtue.
-I see that they have brought one more guest, who not a virtue. Who are you, young lady? - Asked the Chief of the city to Carmi.
-I'm Carmi, respectable sir (bowing). - It was all Carmi could say. The arrival in Atlantis left her even more confused than at first.
-Carmi is a guest of the virtues, we regret not having informed her presence when we arrival.
-She is the opportunity we have to recover Turum and that everything is in order again. We ask that you please welcome her as one more guest. We stand behind her and take responsibility for. She will not cause problems. - Knowledge assured them.

-As for the other virtues, do I have to worry? - Asked the head of Atlantis
-Like us, they would have to request your permission to enter. You can accept or deny their entry; I can't do anything about that. You can receive them if it is your decision; it just seemed to me that after the story of how they ended up at the sea floor and the important role of Justice in that fact, they would not want to receive to him especially. - Knowledge reminded them.

-In that you are right, Knowledge. All the Atlanteans are aware that if it had not been for you and for your intervention with the other virtues, including Justice, Atlantis would have disappeared completely. - The Chief acknowledged.
-Also remember that Atlantis is neutral territory. Even if you receive us, none of you have nothing to do with the conflict that we now have with Justice and company. - Knowledge told him, to reassure him and finish convincing him.

-They can stay as long as they need. We will do everything possible to make your stay with us pleasant. We will host them in our palace. And if something is offered to you, do not hesitate to inform us and we will provide it to you. - The leader offered them to the virtues and to Carmi.

-Thank you very much, Great Chief, but it won't be necessary. With a totally uninhabited and disabled area of the city it will be fine; if it is far from the population it will be better. - Knowledge asked him.

-Okay, then that will. We will be sending food for you and for her guest, she will need the food. And you, in case it is required or you fancy. From somewhere or something they have to obtain and recover energy, if they want to walk around the city, go ahead, that more than anything else would help them to recover their magic. My guards will take you to the place you ask. - The Great Chief indicated. -For now, you can wait in the palace for your partner feel better to leave. She is almost completely restored, so she can go with you too at once. You're welcome all! - The Great Chief finished.

And they took the virtues to a medical wing of the palace to wait for Free Will and take her with them. Now, although it is true that virtues do not get sick, it is because they are maintained with energy thanks to the fact that those virtues are still present in human beings, but by remaining isolated for so long (in a special prison, proof of any magic that does not belonged to Justice), they had the bare minimum, and adding the fact that Free Will was the one that had used their gifts the most to save everyone, ran out of energy. The Atlanteans resorted to food (which they essentially did not need, but in the circumstances, it could be an option).

With food and with the excellent care of the Atlantean doctors, in a few hours Free Will was reestablished, and the virtues immediately went to the place that would them provide in the city.

CHAPTER 11 HISTORY AND MAGIC OF TURUM

That was a wonderful place, full of vast vegetation and even light. At those depths it was impossible for sunlight to filter through, whatever its source of energy and light, it gave the impression of really being natural sunlight. The whole place seemed like a lost paradise like those that existing in the Carmi's dimension; she was fascinated with the place. If it were not because she knew they were in the lost city at the sea floor, she would have believed that she was in one of the beautiful places of protected natural areas that existed in her world.

But there was no time to admire the place much; there were many things to do. And they started. They sat on the green grass (it really was like life on earth, but under the sea, it was amazing) and they told everything to Carmi, well, Knowledge told everything:

"Good, a little over a thousand years ago, we, like any virtue or quality in you world, were still something intangible, only appreciated in the people who owned us. But when we saw what humanity was becoming, how evil was gaining ground, we were too disappointed, so several virtues -including myself-, we decided to leave the dimension in which you live, Carmi, and create in an alternate dimension a new city: Turum. We chose certain human beings to be founding inhabitants of Turum, and once Turum was fully formed, we took them to populate it".

"For centuries we were living in peace, quite pleased with the result of the city. But a couple of centuries ago things started to change, the evil that we thought we had left behind in your dimension finally made its way here as well. So as a measure, knowing that in the process the situation could get a bit worse, and eventually everything would return to its normal course, we decided to ask to Free Will to join the Committee of the 13 virtues: Nobility, Purity, Goodness, Generosity, Bravery, Knowledge, Justice, Volition, Honor, Honesty, Loyalty, and Kindness. As you can notice, one of the virtues is not mentioned, since having field obligations, more than a permanent place, in reality Turum was just founded, she has been traveling around the world and dimensions, so we needed a 13th permanent presence on the Committee".

"Came the day of the arrival of Free Will, or F.W. -as she also likes to be called- and, although Justice at the time expressed his dissatisfaction with her arrival, we thought it was already clear that Free Will would come to Turum and would be part of the Committee, but I was wrong. I underestimated his annoyance and the day F.W. He arrived, in the middle celebration Justice rebelled, at first I thought it was part of the show, but later I realized that was not. I don't know if he had already planned this or not, but several inhabitants seemed to be supporting him, in addition to some virtues. And the rest you already know. "

"But there is a way to get Turum back, and that's where you come in, Carmi. Into the Committee Headquarters building, some urns are remain kept saved that contain a large part of our magic potential, of us, the 13 virtues, but among virtues, we feel our presence, as well as our presence in any of the inhabitants of the city , so we cannot enter the building. They will notice our presence, they know that we can perceive them, and we do not have much support from the population, so none virtue, only one person, who is not from Turum is undetectable, even if he possesses the virtues, and that's the one who could help us ".

"That is why we opened the portal, waiting for someone, especially brave in the first instance, but also possessing the other virtues, would venture to reach the location of the portal that we opened, and decide to cross it, and you appeared. Please don't leave us to our fate, we have exhausted our resources, and without those urns there is no way to deal with the situation. Our relief is that only the virtue that owns each urn is the one who can open it, but Justice being able to dispose of the urns of five other virtues, has the total power of 6 virtues, even without opening ours, and we have only remains of power without those urns. That is a losing battle before it begins".

"Carmi, you will have to enter the Headquarters and take the urns from where he have them and you will bring them to us. That knowing Justice as he is, surely he has already removed them from the vault where they were, and will have them as close as possible to him, surely in the main forum of the Headquarters. And at a certain point, if it becomes necessary, you can and should open them. We will tell you everything you need to know, luck that you are so athletic and know about extreme sports as they call it in your dimension, it saves us a long training that we could not have given you adequately. Rest of the day rest, you will need it, tomorrow we will start your preparation and training". Finished and she prepared to leave Knowledge.

-Wait a moment, Knowledge. I think I remember that you mentioned that only the virtue that owns the urn was who could open it, how is it that you say that at a certain moment if it is required I will open them? I don't understand. - Carmi asked her.

-Is deducted that anyone who is possessor of virtue has the ability to do so, that is why we are the owners the suitables to open them, but any inhabitant of Turum could open them ... if they had the necessary virtues, and with us captives there is no way that none inhabitant of Turum can open them, only the 6 urns of the other virtues. That is why you, being from another dimension that does not depend directly so much on our magic as this city, you and the people of your world are capable of maintaining their virtues without us on the lookout all the time, with our traveler companion hovering around the existing dimensions is more than enough. So right now, it's you, Carmi, the only being who, once we are back in surface of Turum, will have enough potential of each of the virtues that he will be able to open any of the urns without problem. Rest virtues, and Carmi. - Knowledge answered him, and finally withdrew.

The night was near, and as it came, the other virtues used that time to get to know Carmi a little more. Nobility and Bravery especially, made good friends with her. Night also fell on Atlantis and everyone got ready to sleep, it had been a very hectic day, and what awaited them tomorrow was no more peaceful.

CHAPTER 12

Dawn came to Atlantis and with that, Carmi's intensive three-day training. During that time they told and taught her everything she had to know about Turum, more than anything, about the Headquarters Building, how to enter without being seen, and how the building was constituted, the best routes to reach the Justice room and the main forum, and emergency escape routes.

Carmi showed how skillful and agile she was, she learned everything very quickly. And with how well fed they had her; she was very energetic, even the virtues ate a little. Since not all of them were always present at the training sessions, taking advantage of the Great Chief's invitation, they took turns to walk around the city and recharge their strength and their magic thanks to the Atlanteans, and it worked, better than food, they only tried it for not despising their hosts and for accompanying Carmi.

At the end of the training, even Knowledge, who, while not being unfriendly by any means, was quite serious and reserved, was friendlier and open with Carmi. The virtues returned to the main plaza of the Atlantes to thank her for your hospitality and to say goodbye to their. It was time to return to the surface of Turum and restore the city.

-Thank you very much for everything, inhabitants of Atlantis. For receiving us and giving us shelter and protection here, time is short and we cannot stay any longer, duty calls us. I hope to see you again soon, and in more favorable circumstances.- Knowledge finished, bowing.
-Thank you very much for your gooddness and generosity towards us. - Carmi also said goodbye. This farewell caused a little bit of grace to everyone, especially the Great Chief.
-Hahaha, young lady, They precisely did a lot (those virtues), it was partly courtesy of them, so in that we have to thank her companions- he said pointing to where these two virtues were.

And once they said goodbye to the Atlanteans, once again Knowledge requested of Free Will and Purity for find a new safe place for the virtues, while Carmi obtained the urns and gave them to their. The barrier of Atlantis was opened just so that the virtues could pass through and it was sealed again.

Again Knowledge turned to Free Will and also to Purity to find a suitable place on the surface and go directly to that place. Since it was an unknown place even to Knowledge, she left that in hands of the other virtues. It was difficult without knowing the exact place and without coordinates either, but they managed to get closer to the site and it really looked good, so they continued walking and a few meters ahead they were in the place, to tell the truth, all that extension of land could be occupied.

They were behind a wall of trees called "weeping willow"* which with their branches that reached the ground, completely and perfectly covered the space behind. It was an area between wooded and jungle, but apparently uninhabited, only vegetation and some accumulations of stones and rocks. However, Purity and Free Will stopped next to a not very large rock and did not stop looking and touching it.

Both indicated to the other virtues that this was the place and they asked Bravery to do something to allow them to enter the site, and with a contribution of extra force from Free Will, he managed to weaken that area and the rock sank and revealed a cavern large underground. The virtues rushed down with an impressive jump of almost 10 meters to reach the background, but Carmi stayed up until Goodness invited her to go down:

Thank you, just wait a moment, I'll secure a rope and go down.- Carmi told her, and Goodness smiled at her, as if something was amusing, and said:
-That's not necessary Carmi, just jump.-
-It's something high Goodness; it doesn't seem very safe to me, as much as I like adventure and all that stuff. - Carmi replied somewhat skeptically, looking at the space of about 10 meters of depth.
-Don't worry, trust me. Nothing will happen to you. Have faith. - Goodness also encouraged her.

Carmi, with doubts but trusting as they told her, took a "jump of faith" and what happened surprised her. She was prepared to land on the ground, but that did not happen. A meter before arriving she began to stop and ended up walking down slower.
"You're welcome." Free Will told her, who stopped her fall so that nothing would happen to her.
-Thank you F.W.- Carmi said amazed.
"I told you, nothing was going to happen to you." - Goodness reminded her.

And they continued touring the cavern; it would be an excellent place. Besides, they would not stay there long, since Carmi was ready to go to the Headquarters in search of the urns of the Virtues of Turum.

-The only thing we can do now is give you this.- Knowledge said to Carmi, handing her a milky way necklace, which when she saw it in the light of the day and turned it was like seeing a northern lights, she loved it.
-Thank you very much, it's very beautiful, but you didn't have to give me anything. I still don't have the urns. - The young woman thanked them.

-It's good that you liked it, but that's not a necklace, or rather: it's not just a necklace. It has a transporting function to the place where we are. When you already have the urns in your hands, you just have to say or visualize in your mind where you want to go and it will immediately transport you to the desired place. You will ask that take you with us, where we are, be very careful how you use it, since you can only use it once.- Free Will informed her.

-But why? - Carmi asked them
-As we already told you before, we the virtues, perceive us among ourselves, we feel our power, so a strong charge of magic would reveal your presence and we would lose that advantage. The necklace has a certain amount of magic in it, and the same to keep that power hidden, or at a minimum level, so it will be undetectable. When you transport yourself, the necklace will release all the magic and they will realize that someone unexpected has entered, and also that the urns are no longer there, but by then you will be with us and we will have the urns, they will not be able to do anything. And at last there will be the possibility of recovering and saving Turum. Use that necklace wisely, part of the magic of Free Will, Bravery and mine are in it, and there is no second chance. - Knowledge explained.

Having said all this, Free Will got up to the surface with Carmi and took her to a nook just under a kilometer from the Headquarters building and a half a kilometer from the Central Plaza.
-It's the closest I can get you without exposing myself too much, but I have to go before someone notices my presence and they inform someone before you get there. Good luck and success in

your mission, The Virtues and all Turum count on it. We will see you soon. - Free Will said, gave her a hug and left quickly, returning to the cavern with the other virtues.

CHAPTER 13

Now Carmi was completely alone, and she started her way towards the Headquarters building, what she was seeing of Turum seemed like a city with much modernity, but in terms of its architecture, the style of the buildings was more like an old city, but that mix of modern and old styles seemed quite interesting to her. But she had to concentrate, so she followed her path and focused solely on what the virtues indicated to her.

A few meters from reaching the Headquarters Building, Carmi stopped and noticed the surveillance of the place. How useful it would have been if the place had those secret tunnels that many places in her dimension had, but since Turum did not have this, the plan was different. After observing for a few minutes from the top of a tree located in that area, she discovered a blind spot, without any surveillance. The downside is that it was a small window, maybe 30x40 or 45 cm. And she wasn't really sure if she could get in that way, plus she was carrying a backpack, though not very big, maybe wider than the window. And one more drawback: it seemed to be located on the second floor.

Among the things she carried that had given her the virtues (her stuff stayed in the Arch of Time, or so she thought), she looked for something that could help her displace from the tree and open the window, hoping that did not have any protection. Looking for something to lean on to displace, she saw a strange piece that looked like blacksmithing, and of there she secured the rope grab hook, hoping it would be strong enough to support her weight when sliding and be able to reach the window and enter this way to the building.

She slid about 100 meters and managed to get close to the window, almost crashing into the wall, but she managed to get there well, half a meter from where the window was, but it opened on the opposite side. So she had to stretch and slide a little more to reach the part of the window that opened, after a bit of effort she got it and was able to open the window. Now was missing getting inside.

With the help of the lifeline * of her harness she pushed herself up and reached the window, barely holding on. She pushed himself up again and managed to get inside. He got rid of the ropes and the harness (put it away), she almost had to get rid of his backpack, but after a few tugs she got to pass it through the window, just hoped that have enough resources still to get to where the urns of the Virtues were and be able to leave.

She was in a bathroom, and thankfully empty. Now she had to verify that there was no one outside so that she could leave, just as she was about to leave she heard a few steps and locked herself in the bathroom again. She waited a few more minutes until she doesn't hear anything and she checked again. There was no one outside anymore, so she took advantage and left, but she was slow to orient herself from where she was, when she did, continued walking quietly until she heard a few steps again, she hid behind some posts and while was there, she saw the other side to where was, on that same floor the stairs to the third floor, where the vault was, and right next to, the access to the main forum, where Justice was guarding the urns of the Virtues.

How to distract him? How to get him out of the forum? How could she take the urns? As she thought about all this, the necklace she was wearing began to react, and an internal light made it shine. Carmi, realizing that, covered it with her hand so that they would not discover her; the necklace was reacting to the proximity of the urns.

But not only the necklace reacted, also the urns of Bravery and Knowledge began to give off a certain light, of course by feeling the magic (although scarce) of these virtues, which contained the necklace, luckily the urn of Free Will could not be used and for that reason it did not shine, but with those two it was enough to attract Justice's attention.

At this point Carmi was in a gap located between the stairs and the access to the forum, to hide in what she thought of as taking the urns. But at that moment she hears a deafening scream, was Justice:
-Guards! Come right now! -
-Tell us Justice, what can we do for you? - One of them asked him, the one who came first to his call.
-Can they do something right?! Bravery and Knowledge, at least, have managed to enter the building and you have allowed it! Find them immediately and bring them to me! Right away! Move! - Justice yelled outrageously, he seemed to be out of his mind.

The guards of the building mobilized immediately, Justice provided them with special equipment to capture them (not kill them), since only one virtue could fight against another virtue. If the virtues had regained their magic and decided to appear in the Headquarters building that only meant that this time they were willing to use it to reach Justice and take the urns from him.

Once they left, Justice opened the safe located in the forum and removed the urns and left them in view of everyone right there, if they wanted them so much, that them go for them, to see what happened first, if they captured Bravery and Knowledge (and some other virtue that would have entered as well) or if they came directly and by their own foot to the forum to take the urns.

CHAPTER 14

As soon as Free Will arrived back to the cavern, the other virtues were already waiting for her to decide the next step.

-We can't leave her alone for long; she needs us there as soon as she has the urns in her hands. It's the surprise factor, whether he does not realize when she takes them, or she can barely leave the headquarters and Justice already realizes everything, it is the best time to reappear in front of all Turum, and use the power of the urns if that becomes necessary. - Bravery expressed them.

-Yes. It seems somewhat risky, but it is certainly the best option. - Knowledge approved.
-Are you serious? - Asked surprised and excited Bravery.
-So seriously. But you don't get too used to that. - Replied with a smile Knowledge, it was very rare for her to smile, but since Carmi's arrival, seemed that she did it a little more. - Virtues, do you also agree with Bravery? - She asked the others.
They all nodded at the same time.

-In that case, the most convenient thing is leave as soon as possible... Justice surely already realized that someone entered the headquarters building without authorization and Carmi may need us. Let's go now, but we must keep our distance from the Headquarters and the Plaza, but stay close. - Knowledge informed them.

-When we feel that the magic of the necklace is released we all have to go immediately to the Plaza to see Carmi there, and let all in Turum see us.- Bravery told them, Knowledge nodded, and then the other virtues.

They moved at high speed almost as if they were floating in the air (all virtues had that ability). And in a matter of a few minutes they reached the surroundings of the Plaza, scattered, of course, and waited for the magic of the necklace to be released, to meet in the center of the Plaza. A few minutes passed and nothing happened, this began to worry them and Bravery began to advance, but Goodness, who was close to him, stopped him, and they hid together.

Meanwhile Carmi, who had taken advantage of the entrance of the guards to the forum to be able to enter herself, hid behind one of the pillars inside the forum, she was advancing little by little to get closer to where the urns were, but she could not find the right way to get close enough to take them away without being discovered.

She was looking among the things she had in the backpack, she missed her backpack so much, she would surely have found something more appropriate in that. In this case there was not much to help her with. Looking a little more, she managed to find something and made use of the vandalism teachings of television and made a homemade bomb that caused an explosion strong enough to draw the attention of Justice to the access of the forum, who immediately moved to see who had caused such a noise.

It was at that moment that Carmi took advantage and ran with all her might towards the urns with the backpack ready and covering the urns with it, she put them away and was ready to take them away, but when she got up and ran, with the backpack she made a noise and Justice he turned to her in surprise and fury. Young Carmi panicked, however her survival instinct was stronger. She remembered her necklace and immediately said: Take me to where the virtues. And the necklace released all the magic and a strong light and energy field, pushing Justice away when he seemed to reach for her.

Carmi disappeared instantly and when the light stopped dazzling her she realized that she was in the Plaza that she had seen when Free Will left her nearby and left. With the difference that now F.W. and the other Virtues she had known were also there, waiting for her, as when she passed through the portal and reached Turum.

Meanwhile Justice went mad from the forum and called all the guards, watchmen, soldiers, and every warrior he counted on, those who had not gone in search of the Virtues and had stayed in the building, in addition to the Virtues who they supported him, to go in search of Carmi and the fugitive Virtues. He only said: The fugitives have returned! Capture them! NOW! And communicate it to those who left- After, looking at the Virtues, he said: -You, come with me, we know where you are, now we can feel your presence. - And he said at the battle cry addressing everyone: - EVERYONE TO THE PLAZA!

And they started their way, Justice and the virtues arrived in a matter of seconds, of course, thanks to their great speed, and the others were on their way, and the place was not very far. When they were in the Plaza, all the Virtues met face to face, after just over a year.

CHAPTER 15

Carmi reappeared in the Plaza and there were the Virtues, who looked relieved to see her safe and sound. Everyone - including Knowledge - went to greet her and hug her, happy to see that everything had apparently turned out well.
-We are glad to see you well. Did you get the urns? - Knowledge asked her.
-Here they are- Carmi replied, handing her the backpack with the urns. But one was missing.

Just at that moment, before they took the backpack, Justice and the Virtues that accompanied him arrived at the place and Bravery pushed Carmi out of the way to protect her. Finally, Nobility, Purity, Goodness, Generosity, Bravery, Knowledge, Free Will, Justice, Volition, Honor, Honesty, Loyalty and Kindness were reunited. It was a very tense moment, and Carmi could only be a spectator from a distance, unable to do anything else.

-It's a pleasure to see you again ... partners (and he seeing Bravery). - Justice greeted.
-Justice, I see that the new provisions in Turum have resulted ... not as you expected, I dare say- Knowledge told him.
-Since ... You left the fortress it is not that someone have done too much, other than hide ... and bring this young foreign girl to the city. Carmi, right? -He protested and asked, looking towards where the young woman was.
-I was wondering where the owner of the objects we found in the Arc was and when she would appear here. - He continued talking and holding in his hand Carmi's identification, which was in the luggage that had been left in the tunnel of the Arc of Time.
-So she was her best option? If they were going to bring someone from the other dimension, you would have chosen better - Justice continued, to bother.
-She went through the portal, the portal chose her, and you know that," Purity replied very annoyed.

-A foreigner will never be able to understand what Turum is or respect it, no matter how much the portal has let her cross. - Spoke Honor, defensively.
-And yet here she is, risking herself for a place and for unknown people. She is able to see how important Turum is to us, which is our home- Generosity defended her.
-You said it, Generosity: OUR HOME. Not that of an ordinary foreign thief, who cannot even do well what they are entrusted to do- Justice said with disdain as he held his own urn with one hand and showed them to everyone.
-Did you really believe that I would have my own neglected urn, at the mercy of you, or of her savior? -He told them with a scathing tone, before everyone's astonished gaze.

-It's true that now they have their urns and ours. However, our magic remains strong thanks to the inhabitants of Turum, we are even able to equalize its power with the urns and with my urn in my possession, I can double it. So you better give up now, I promise to give you a better deal in your prison. They will be treated as my guests rather than as prisoners. - Justice assured them, with a more amiable tone.

-Avoid unnecessary fighting. After all, we are all virtues; we all want the best for Turum. Knowledge, realize that Justice is right, as well as Honesty and I did it, and do not complicate things, I repeat, it is something unnecessary. - Said almost pleading Kindness.

But was too late to turn back, the fate of everyone in Turum was at stake, and an opportunity like the one that presented itself now, even if it+ was minimal, was hardly going to be repeated again, at least in the short or medium term, too long for the life expectancy of the inhabitants of Turum. So, fearful for the first time in millennia, Knowledge steeled herself (thanks probably also to Bravery, who was by her side) and replied to Justice and company:

-Fighting for the good of Turum is not unnecessary, quite the opposite. So it's our decision to continue with this.

The other virtues that accompanied Knowledge stood to one side of her, showing their support, and holding hands. Then a strange glow emerged from Carmi's backpack, and she turned around immediately since she did not understand what was happening, Free Will told her to calm down, that everything would be fine, what happened is that LA was, when taking the virtues of the hand, opening the urns from a distance, and unlocking the potential of contained magic. Justice and company did some too, they recharging themselves through the inhabitants of Turum, as he had well said; they brought them an enormous amount of magic.

Once all the virtues recharged with magic, what Justice and Honor did is create a huge force field and launch it towards Knowledge and company, but between Knowledge, Bravery and Free Will they contained and diverted it, destroying the Main Plaza. Nobility, Purity, Goodness and Generosity drove Carmi away from the place and protected her, they were barely narrowly spared. By now, due to the noise, they had already attracted the attention of the population of the city. The situation was already getting more and more complicated. That is why Goodness told to Carmi:

-Carmi, please, do something to make this madness stop, we -thanks to the urns- can create a kind of shield for Turum, or by telepathy move the population away from this area, but sooner or later the magic will run out, and we do not know how long Knowledge, Bravery and Free Will can continue to contain the attacks of Justice and the others. Eventually we will meet with Knowledge and by doing that the population would be left unprotected, and we don't want that. Please, the portal chose you for something, you are special, HELP US!!! - Goodness pleaded with Carmi.

Immediately Nobility, Purity, Goodness and Generosity returned where the other virtues were and began to create protection for the inhabitants of Turum, and by telepathy, directing them to safe havens. Although Thanks to the many abilities of Free Will they could skillfully channel and direct part of the magic and gifts of all the virtues (which was at that time her main contribution), there would be a time when they could not do it anymore, and they would need to be all the united virtues, in order to be more efficient and that F.W. could use other gifts.

Volition, Honesty, Loyalty, Kindness tried to block the gifts of the girls to destroy the protection of the city. And just when they seemed to be on par, Loyalty captured the girls, leaving them in a transparent cylindrical prison that Justice had made next to the Headquarters building (with the same quality of blocking the magic of virtues), and the shield and telepathy were broke up.

Carmi, seeing all this, and desperate to help, although she did not know how, the only thing that occurred to her was one thing: destroy all the urns. She did not know that would happen once this was done, the virtues did not even mention that, only that if necessary, when the time came, she was able to open all the urns. But she needed the urn of Justice. She tried to communicate telepathically with Purity and the others so that they could somehow take it for her, but they didn't respond.

Then Carmi ran and in a remote area tried to break the urns, slammed them against the ground, but nothing happened, they were intact, they seemed made of a material similar to ivory or granite, but no matter how hard she tried to break them, absolutely nothing happened, she proceeded to open one and did it without problems, and a glow even more intense than when F.W. she opened them, freed itself, then she closed it again, but she couldn't break them.

She realized that this light had attracted attention, and that a mature man and a woman a few years younger than the man, but also mature, went out in search of her (Loyalty and Honesty). She fled the place as fast as she could, in search of a hammer or some other tool that could help her break the urns, but it was useless, she found nothing, and the virtues found her.

They tried to take Carmi's backpack, but, not having all the qualities, they could not take it, the magic of the other virtues rejected them (Justice used a special kind of spell-glove to can touch the urns), so if only Carmi could take them, they would take Carmi with them.

Loyalty and Honesty brought Carmi in the presence of Justice, in front of the astonished and disconcerting gaze of Knowledge and company, and the combat stopped at that moment.
-We have found the urns - Loyalty informed to Justice and to his companions.

Justice turned to see the young woman with the backpack on her back.
-Do you realize, so many attempts to restore the old order in Turum, and to protect this girl, all were in vain? - Justice snapped at Knowledge and her allies.
Justice took Carmi's backpack and put all the urns together, including his.
-Thank you very much for your contribution, young lady. It was all that was required of you. Now, my faithful warriors, lock her up with the other virtues! - And two soldiers took her away.

On the way Carmi realized that very close to where they were passing was a dock, and there, a huge ship (a kind of ark or cruise ship), and taking advantage of her strength and that the soldiers were human, like her. She hit one, took the gun from his and with it hit the other and ran as fast as she could, heading for the dock.

Once there, although she had never driven anything, a lot less a boat or ship, of course, there was a paper in front of the commandos, as a kind of quick guide. Carmi turned it on and put it at full speed. From a distance she saw that the situation was at a disadvantage for Knowledge, Bravery and Free Will, not having to Nobility, Purity, Goodness and Generosity. So, without thinking about it, she out with the ship, heading exactly where the Virtues were, but before arriving, she veered towards the place where all the urns were, it was the upper part of a kind of water source, she came out towards the edge of the ship and jumped just before crashing it into the fountain, thus destroying the urns, and causing an explosion and fire in the place. The magic of all the virtues stopped for a moment and they were displaced by the explosion. A blinding glow emanated from the place where the urns had been before and were now destroyed.

Something akin to a fire alarm went off in the city and city fire trucks reached what was left of the Main Plaza. Carmi got up with some scratches and bruises, but still with strength, she realized that an urn had survived, she spotted an ax in a fire truck, and went to take it, with the urn in one hand, and crawling a little in the walking, she took the ax between her hands, and with all the strength she had left, she destroyed the urn that remained.

Doing so released a glow and a force field (like what happened with the Milky Way necklace, but stronger and more intense) threw her away, knocking her unconscious for a few moments, but what happened then, was amazing.

CHAPTER 16

When the last urn was destroyed, the sky opened, the clouds cleared everything and someone appeared, flying, descending towards the place, at that moment Carmi woke up and saw what was happening. A dove that got bigger and bigger as it went down, until transformed into a young woman, about 25 human years old, between 1.55-1.60m tall, thin, wavy light brown hair, light skin and big black eyes, dressed with a white tailored suit, with a kind of tail at the back of the coat, with sleeves and pants flared in the lower.

-They really have made a mess here; I can't leave them alone for a few centuries without I being necessary, right? - The traveling virtue told them with a certain air of humor.
-Hope, what are you doing here? - Justice asked her, standing up, while the other virtues did as well.
-Well, some too insistent calls for help came to my ears from here in Turum, but apparently it wasn't from an inhabitant of Turum, which caught my attention, it seems to me that they were originally for Nobility, Purity, or one of the girls, but for some reason, couldn't reach the original addressee, like some other calls that I have been hearing for some time. - answered HOPE, THE VIRTUE NUMBER 13, to him.

-Knowledge, old friend, you don't have the best look that you've ever had. Truth be told, none of you, Virtues, look very good. So you are the young woman who asked for help, what's your name? - Hope asked.
-I'm Carmi - she replied, reincorporating from the ground, already very weak.
- I officially introduce myself. I'm Hope, the 13th virtue, I suppose you heard something of me, my work is mainly in the field. - And she went down to where Carmi was, shaking her hand. When Carmi greeted her, Hope took her with both hands and a healing force emanated from her and Carmi was completely and surprisingly healed when they let go.

-I see they finally destroyed the urns, they know it never seemed like a good idea to me, having that stored power could cause a pitched battle at some point- Hope continued.
-Justice, that temperament of yours, my friend, always creating controversies. Was necessary?-
-Maybe not, maybe I overdid it, we needed you, travel woman." Justice replied with a slight smile. At that moment, Justice disabled the prison and destroyed it, so Nobility, Purity, Goodness and Generosity were free again, and they came to meet with the other virtues.

- HOPE?! - The 4 exclaimed in unison.
- Nice to see you girls again - She said smiling.
None of the virtues seemed to understand the behavior that Justice and Hope showed, Carmi did not understand either. At that moment Justice approached where Hope was and Carmi, Knowledge and the other virtues rushed to protect their, but Hope stopped them. Then Justice went to Carmi and repeated: -Thank you very much for her contribution, young lady. It was all that was required of you. - And he added before passing by: - CONGRATULATIONS! We hope to have good news from you in the future, and have a happy return to your dimension on Earth.- He told her this, he gave her a slight smile, and left, bowing to Hope.

Loyalty handed to Carmi the suitcase with her belongings back, bowed briefly, and withdrew from the place behind Justice. In the midst of great confusion, it was all over, finally.

CHAPTER 17

After all the disaster caused, the 13 virtues met behind closed doors in what was left of the Headquarters Building, to talk ALL with Hope, the only ones who seemed to know what had happened were mainly Hope, Justice and to some extent, Loyalty. A couple of hours later, all the virtues came out, without saying anything, and began to rebuild and repair the damage that Turum had suffered. Hope in her dove form flew around the city and healed the wounded (thanks to the shield made by the corresponding virtues, there was no loss of life to mourn, but were several wounded).

They used what was left of the day, and part of the next day, before noon it was all as if nothing had happened. Carmi stayed to sleep in one of the rooms that were in the Headquarters Building once it was repaired, finally, no virtue was actually sleeping, so there was no problem for that, also they were very busy, they could not sleep even if they were able to do it and wanted.

Just arrived the noon, the at that time 14 virtues were reunited, all again wearing gala dresses and suits, but this time without the terrible end that had the previous occasion that they used them, in the arrival of Free Will to the city.

Hope wore a suit for that occasion exactly the same style as the one she wore when she returned to Turum, but combined in white and gold. All the virtues and the inhabitants of the city of Turum gathered in the restored and improved Main Plaza, and said goodbye Carmi. Hope gave the speech on that occasion.

- In the name of the virtues and all the inhabitants of Turum, I want to thank you for the great work done for the well-being of everyone here, and I wanted to give you a gift as a thank you.- She said this taking Carmi's hands in hers. A force was released from her, and Carmi felt it inside her, giving her enormous strength and peace that she felt instantly, and a tear rolled down her cheek.
- This feeling, what is this?" Carmi asked Hope.
-It's hope, which was what called me back to Turum, what caused that you can to destroy the urns, and what finally saved the city and everyone. Say by there: while there is life, there is hope, and it's that hope what you will never lack, the one that will sustain you in difficult moments and the one that will make you emerge victorious from any situation, because while you have hope, all the other virtues of being human, will always be inside you, and they will help you to be the best human being that you are destined to be in your world. - Hope replied.

-Well, as you know, my main task is around the existing world, -continued Hope - I can't stay in one place for long, so I will go too, but remember that I'm always with you, keep it always in mind. And after the recent events and having fixed some existing differences, everything will improve here in Turum. In addition, I promise to visit more often, so that the other virtues of the committee and you, dear inhabitants, don't miss me - and she winked and smiled at the committee.

- SEE YOU VERY SOON, HAVE A WONDERFUL AND SATISFACTORY EXISTENCE - told Hope everyone in the Plaza, and made a great bow to the committee and the population. Free Will approached Hope and Carmi, the three held of their hands and while Hope flew away just like she arrived, left go her hand and turned into a dove again, and Free Will was transported herself along with Carmi towards the portal of the arc, not without first Carmi looking back and saying goodbye to all the virtues and friends that she left there as they advanced.

They finally reached the arc, and Free Will said goodbye giving Carmi a big hug.
- What will happen with you, F.W.? - The young woman asked somewhat worriedly.
-Don't worry - Said smiling F.W. - I'll be fine here, Turum is now my new home, Justice shouldn't worry you, if that's why you're asking. Everything is now clear and we are at peace.
-Okay, thank you very much for everything, it has been an experience that I will never forget. I hope to see you all again! - Carmi said happily.
- We will miss you, but it seems to me that for your own wellness, and that of Turum, you should ideally not try to return here. - The portals can now be closed again - F.W. told her with some sadness.
- I understand, we must protect the existence of Turum from anyone outsider the place, for the good of Turum and my dimension - the young Carmi answered resigned, although somewhat sad too.

And Carmi walked through the portal, and finally was back at the Arc of Time.

EPILOGUE

-CAN WE GO BACK NOW?! WE ARE ALREADY TWO HOURS DELAYED, WE SHOULD HAVE LEFT HERE AT 10AM, AND IT IS ALREADY TWELVE! - The other passengers on the tour were unhappy.

The coordinator, somewhat nervous at this point, was going to speak, but then his cell phone rang, it was Carmi:
-Carmina! Where are you? Have you already realized what time it is? -He said desperate to the phone.
-I know, I'm sorry, really. I'm a bit stuck on something, follow go ahead, I will arrive to the final station, don't worry, and thank you very much.- Carmi replied, and she hung up, leaving him with the word in his mouth.
-This little woman can really be a headache sometimes. - The coordinator told himself, and he headed with the other passengers, and called them to get on the bus and go back.

A few hours later they arrived back, they were already late, and Carmi's parents knew that, but when they saw the bus arrive and did not see their daughter get off, they began to get nervous. They immediately approached the coordinator throwing him many questions: Where was Carmi? Why didn't she come with them? Did something happen to her? The poor coordinator was so nervous.

-W .. Well, what happens is that ... -HERE I AM FAMILY! Did you miss me? -She said hugging and hanging on the back of her parents the young woman.
-Carmi! What a joy to see you again! We did not see you go down and we were worried about you- her mother replied.
-I was just struggling a little bit to get my luggage out of the bus storage; it was left to the bottom, that's all. Don't exaggerate- she said reassuring them and kissing them both on the cheek.

-Well, let's go home, I'm very tired from the trip, and I want to sleep, at least 24 hours, hahaha. Thanks friend, an excellent tour, I did not expect less from you. - And she hugged the coordinator, and went with her parents, before the astonished look of her friend.

(Flashback)
-God! Even if I take the closest bus to departure, and even if my friend's bus stops, and I take in a direct bus, I won't be able to catch up with them, and my parents will know out and I'll be in trouble.- Carmi said somewhat disappointed as she dropped her luggage carelessly on the floor, then he heard something fall out of it, and saw that it was a beige envelope with a Milky Way necklace, like the one Knowledge had given him to escape the Headquarters Building in Turum, and a note too(When F.W. said goodbye, she put it in her luggage without her noticing), which read as follows:

"Dear Carmi, there are no words or enough thanks for what you did, for your bravery. So I wanted to give you as to personal mode, a memory of your stay with us, I think you remember what it is. It can save you from the odd setback, has more than enough magic to last your whole life, use it wisely.

With love.

Free Will (or F.W. for friends, like you).

P.S. I really hope I never have to see you again. "

Carmi went to the bathroom with her luggage, put on the necklace, made sure that no one else was in the bathroom, and said: -Take me back home- a glow came out and Carmi was in her city, she went to see her friend the coach to her house, she told her what happened (not all), that she left with everyone and when arrived she made her own way, her coach reprimanded her, but was happy to see her safe and sound, she took a shower and ate something light with her, already that she had to return to the station to "arrive with the others."

(End of flashback)

Carmi was in her bedroom, lying on her bed, looking at the necklace F.AW. gave her. She'd loved it. How far could she go? How far could her necklace transport her? And she smiled, seeing the necklace.

GLOSSARY (just the words signed with this *):

Unless clarification is made, definitions obtained from the Dictionary of "Oxford Languages".

Crusades: each of a series of medieval military expeditions made by Europeans to recover the Holy Land from the Muslims in the 11th, 12th, and 13th centuries.

Hiking: the activity of going for long walks, especially in the country or woods.

Rappelling: (rapel to go down a very steep slope by holding on to a rope that is fastened to the top of the slope. * (Cambrige Dictionary).

Climbing: the sport or activity of ascending mountains or cliffs.

Kayak: Sports canoe, made of a very light material, with one or more central openings in the deck for the crew, which sails propelled by very wide bladed oars not attached to the hull of the ship. (Translation of Oxford Languages).

Carabiner: a coupling link with a safety closure, used by rock climbers.

Harness: a piece of equipment with straps and belts, used to control or hold in place a person, animal, or object. *(Cambrige Dictionary).

Promontory: a point of high land that juts out into a large body of water; a headland.

ATLANTIS: Atlantis is the name of a mythical island mentioned and described in the dialogues Timaeus and Critias, texts by the Greek philosopher Plato. In these dialogues, the island appears as a military power that existed nine thousand years before the time of the Athenian legislator Solon.* (Traslation of Wikipedia)

Atlantes: adj. Of or pertaining to the mythical continent of Atlantis. m. and f. Inhabitant of the mythical continent of Atlantis.* (Translation of Oxford Languages)

Weeping Willow: (SALIX BABYLONICA) a Eurasian willow with trailing branches and foliage reaching down to the ground, widely grown as an ornamental in waterside settings.

Lifeline: a rope or line used for life-saving, typically one thrown to rescue someone in difficulties in water or one used by sailors to secure themselves to a boat.